WELCOME TO PASSPORT TO READING

A beginning reader's ticket to a brand-new world!

Every book in this program is designed to build read-along and read-alone skills, level by level, through engaging and enriching stories. As the reader turns each page, he or she will become more confident with new vocabulary, sight words, and comprehension.

These PASSPORT TO READING levels will help you choose the perfect book for every reader.

READING TOGETHER
Read short words in simple sentence structures together to begin a reader's journey.

READING OUT LOUD
Encourage developing readers to sound out words in more complex stories with simple vocabulary.

READING INDEPENDENTLY
Newly independent readers gain confidence reading more complex sentences with higher word counts.

READY TO READ MORE
Readers prepare for chapter books with fewer illustrations and longer paragraphs.

This book features sight words from the educator-supported Dolch Sight Words List. This encourages the reader to recognize commonly used vocabulary words, increasing reading speed and fluency.

For more information, please visit passporttoreadingbooks.com.

Enjoy the journey!

Cover design by Ching Chan.

Little, Brown and Company
Hachette Book Group
1290 Avenue of the Americas, New York, NY 10104
Visit us at LBYR.com
First Edition: February 2019

Little, Brown and Company is a division of Hachette Book Group, Inc.
The Little, Brown name and logo are trademarks of Hachette Book Group, Inc.

The publisher is not responsible for websites (or their content) that are not owned by the publisher.

ISBNs: 978-0-316-41482-1 (pbk.), 978-0-316-41479-1(ebook),
978-0-316-41483-8 (ebook), 978-0-316-41477-7 (ebook)

PRINTED IN THE UNITED STATES OF AMERICA

CW

10 9 8 7 6 5 4 3 2 1

Passport to Reading titles are leveled by independent reviewers applying the standards developed by Irene Fountas and Gay Su Pinnell in *Matching Books to Readers: Using Leveled Books in Guided Reading*, Heinemann, 1999.

Meet the Crew!

Story adapted by Trey King

LB
LITTLE, BROWN AND COMPANY
New York Boston

Attention, **Wonder Park** friends!
Look for these words when you
read this book.
Can you spot them all?

amusement

copilot

porcupine

marker

Hi, there!
My name is **June**,
and I like to build things.

Today I am building
an amusement park.
It is called Wonderland.

My favorite tool
is my imagination,
but I cannot create
Wonderland all by myself.
I need my friends to help!

Mom and **Dad** are
always there for me.
Dad is great at giving hugs
and smiling.

And Mom helps me
put my ideas on paper.

Banky is my best friend.

He is an amazing builder
and an awesome copilot.

Of course,
some of my best friends
are also the best helpers.

BOOMER

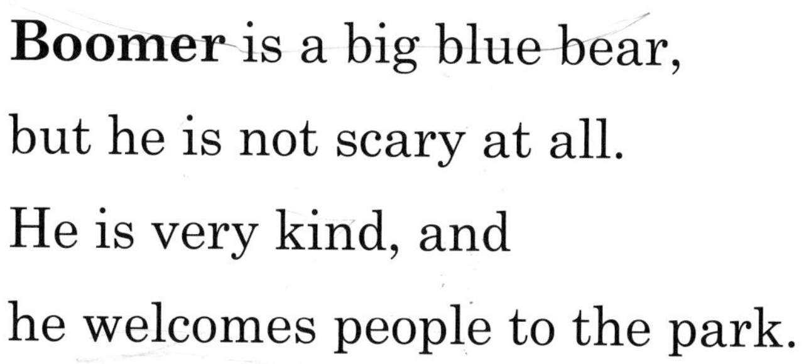

Boomer is a big blue bear,
but he is not scary at all.
He is very kind, and
he welcomes people to the park.

GRETA

Greta is a brave boar.
She is also a team leader
who works hard to keep
everyone together and happy.

Have you ever met a porcupine?
Well, meet **Steve**!
He is in charge of
keeping everyone safe.

He talks a lot and
has a crush on Greta.
But his plans never work out
the way he wants.

GUS & COOPER

These two beavers are
Gus and **Cooper**.
They are good at building things.
That is, when they stay focused.
Gus and Cooper can get
distracted sometimes.

Peanut is the official mascot of Wonderland.
With his magic marker,
he brings my ideas to life!

PEANUT

I had better not forget
the park toys:
the **Wonder Chimp dolls**.

They may look sweet now,
but they can be trouble, too!

It took a lot of work
to create Wonderland.

And I could not have done it without my friends!

With their help,
I can create anything.
Welcome to Wonderland!

What should my friends
and I make next?
Whatever it is,
I know it will be amazing!